*For Carol, John, Sarah, Becky, Rachel, Joel, Elena, Lydia,*
*Katie and Amy* ∞ *P. R.*

*For my Uncle Leo, Aunt Ruth and their thirteen children:*
*John, Richard, William, Rosemary, Albert, Edith,*
*Stephen, David, Mildred, Dolores, Margaret,*
*Alma and Anna – thanks for wonder-filled*
*days down on the farm* ∞ *W. H.*

First published 2000 by Walker Books Ltd
87 Vauxhall Walk, London SE11 5HJ

This edition published 2002

10 9 8 7 6 5 4 3

Text © 2000 Phyllis Root
Illustrations © 2000 Will Hillenbrand

This book has been typeset in Throhand Ink
The pictures were done in mixed media on vellum

Printed in Hong Kong

British Library Cataloguing in Publication Data:
a catalogue record for this book is available
from the British Library

ISBN 0-7445-8915-0

# Kiss the Cow!

WRITTEN BY
## Phyllis Root

ILLUSTRATED BY
## Will Hillenbrand

WALKER BOOKS
AND SUBSIDIARIES
LONDON · BOSTON · SYDNEY

MAMA MAY lived where the earth met the sky,
and her house was as wide as the prairie.

It needed to be.

Mama May had so many children she couldn't count them all. Among Mama May's children was one called Annalisa. She wasn't the youngest and she wasn't the oldest, but she was the most curious and the most stubborn.

Every day Annalisa followed Mama May as
she carried her two shiny milk pails to the meadow
where she kept Luella, her magic cow with the
beautiful brown eyes and bright curving horns.
Every day Annalisa heard Mama May
sing to Luella,

*Lovely Luella,*
*Your milk never fails.*
*My children are hungry,*
*So please fill my pails.*

Every day Annalisa saw Luella's warm
sweet milk flow into the shiny pails
until Mama May sang,

*Thank you, Luella,*
*My children shall eat*
*Cheese fresh and yellow*
*Milk warm and sweet.*

And every day Annalisa saw Mama
May kiss Luella right on the end
of her velvety brown nose.

"Ughhh!"
said Annalisa.
"Imagine kissing
a cow!"

Every day
Mama May carried
her pails of milk home
to feed her hungry children.

One pail of milk they drank for breakfast.

The other pail of milk Mama May heated
and salted and pressed into cheese for
the children's supper, cheese so fresh
it squeaked between
their teeth.

Every day Annalisa wondered, *What would it be like to milk a magic cow?* The more she wondered, the more curious she grew. And the more curious she grew, the more Annalisa just had to know.

Finally one day she said, "I want to milk Luella." "Never you mind about milking Luella," said Mama May. "If you upset her, she'll never give milk again, and then what would we do?"

But Annalisa had made up her mind.
She took a little bucket and slipped
off alone to the meadow.

Just like Mama May, Annalisa sang,

*Lovely Luella,*
*Your milk never fails.*
*My children are hungry,*
*So please fill my pails.*

Luella's milk flowed into Annalisa's
little bucket until she sang,

*Thank you, Luella,*
*My children shall eat*
*Cheese fresh and yellow*
*Milk warm and sweet.*

(Now this wasn't exactly true, of course,
but magic words are magic words,
and, true or not, they worked.)

But did Annalisa kiss Luella right on the end of her soft silky nose?

She did not.

And the next day Luella would not give any milk at all,
no matter how many times Mama May sang her magic song.
It didn't take Mama May long to guess what had happened.

"Annalisa!" she cried. "Have you been bothering Luella?"
"All I did was milk her with my little bucket," said Annalisa.
"And did you remember to kiss the cow?" asked Mama May.
"Me? Kiss a slobbery bristly cow?" cried Annalisa.
"You must kiss the cow to make sure she gives milk again,"
   said Mama May.

"Never!" cried Annalisa.
   And she wouldn't.

That day the children ate scraps of bread without milk for breakfast.

"Now will you kiss the cow?" asked Mama May.

"Never!" said Annalisa.

No kiss, no milk.

That night the children ate crusts of bread without cheese for supper.

"Now will you kiss the cow?" asked Mama May.

"Never!" said Annalisa.

No kiss, no milk, no cheese. The next day Mama May's house
was full of hungry crying children.

The hungry children crowded round Annalisa.
There were so many children they crowded
her right out of the house and
up the hill to the meadow.
"Milk!" they begged.
"Cheese!" they pleaded.

"Now will you kiss the cow?"
asked Mama May.
"Never!" cried Annalisa.
"Never, never, never."

"Moooooooooooo," said Luella,
putting her nose in Annalisa's face.
"Ugh!" said Annalisa.

But then she looked into Luella's beautiful brown eyes

and wondered, *What would it be like to kiss a cow?*

The more she wondered, the more curious she grew.

And the more curious she grew,

the more Annalisa just had to know.

There was only one way to find out.

"Please kiss the cow," said Mama May.

"Hmmmm,"
said Annalisa.

But she scrunched up her eyes,

bunched up her face and kissed Luella.

Luella smelled of fresh hay and sunshine and clover.

Her nose felt silky and warm and dry.

Mama May sang her magic song.

Luella's milk began to flow.

The children cheered.

And Annalisa felt so fine ...

she kissed
the cow
again.

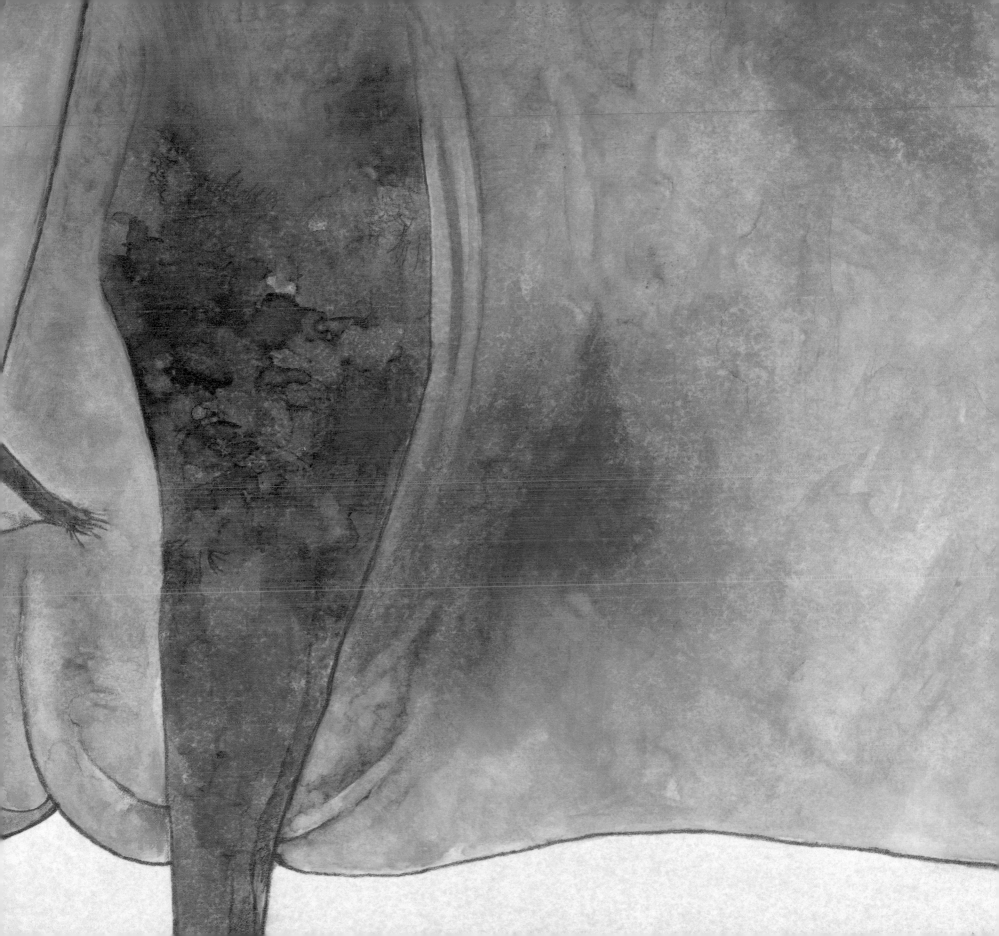

PHYLLIS ROOT says that while writing **Kiss the Cow**, she decided
to do some research. "I went to an agricultural fair and there were all these kids
who were so proud of their cows. I had every intention of kissing a cow,
but it just didn't feel respectful to ask!"

Phyllis Root is the author of many popular picture books including
*Mrs Potter's Pig*, *What Baby Wants*, *One Duck Stuck*, *All for the Newborn Baby*
and *Rattletrap Car*, as well as the Bonnie Bumble stories *Meow Monday*,
*Turnover Tuesday*, *One Windy Wednesday* and *Foggy Friday*.
She lives in Minnesota, USA.

WILL HILLENBRAND decided that he too should try to kiss a cow
while working on this book. "I was willing," he recalls, "but the cow wasn't."

Will Hillenbrand is an acclaimed illustrator of many books for children,
including *Counting Crocodiles* by Judy Sierra and *The Last Snake in Ireland*
by Sheila MacGill-Callahan, as well as his own story, *Down by the Station*.
Will lives in Ohio, USA with his wife and son.